War takes its toll....

Sometimes at night when sleep wouldn't take me, I could still smell the bloodied corpses of our dead and the VC dead rotting in the tropical heat—truth be told, most of my nights were sleepless since returning to the world a year ago.

The Seattle cops were no different than the VC. They hid like scared rabbits when I zapped a few of them, too.

I picked at the remains of the roast beef sub I had set next to the rifle and stuffed the chunks of dry bread and grilled beef, coated in tangy barbecue sauce, into my mouth. The tang of the barbecue sauce livened my taste buds. The Blue Diner still made the best subs in Seattle. I had lost thirty pounds during my tour in 'Nam, but the Seattle diet had helped me to regain some of the loss.

Total War

Russ Crossley

Published by
53rd Street Publishing

Gibsons, British Columbia and Lincoln City, Oregon

53RD STREET PUBLISHING

Dedication

This book is dedicated to my father, his brother, my father-in-law and my wife's Uncles who served in World War II. They sacrificed their youth so that we may enjoy our freedom.

Acknowledgments

Thanks as always must go to my brilliant editor, Colleen Kuehne, who makes these stories better and fixes my inevitable mistakes. Thanks for making me look good, Colleen.

Also by Russ Crossley

Total War

Russ Crossley

Published by 53rd Street Publishing
Copyright 2015 Russ Crossley
All rights reserved

Cover art © G. K. | Dreamstime.com
Cover designed by R. Edgewood
Cover design and layout copyright 2015 by 53rd Street
Publishing
ISBN 978-1-927621-43-1

53rd Street Publishing
Head office: Gibsons B.C. Canada
www.53rdstreetpublishing.com

Table of Contents

Introduction

Union Army General William Tecumseh Sherman once said, "War is hell." yet he is viewed by many historians as an advocate for total war. Total war is war not only against an enemy army but also includes a civilian population as a military target. The idea is to crush morale and support for the war being fought so the enemy army will capitulate thus saving lives.

Of course such tactics have never met with much success, at least that I can see. Think about the London blitz or the German assault of Leningrad during the early days of World War Two, these actions didn't encourage surrender in fact they stiffened resolve.

A less known quote from General Sherman reveals how he truly felt about total war. "I confess, without shame, that I am sick and tired of fighting — its glory is all moonshine; even success the most brilliant is over dead and mangled bodies..." General Sherman understood the impact of total war on people.

The five stories in this collection are about ordinary people who have suffered during war or who experience small victories magnified by the bloody conflicts they are asked to face head on.

I hope you enjoy these stories and that they make you think about war and the people who fought them.

Introduction to Muggins Rules

THIS STORY WAS WRITTEN FOR AN ANTHOLOGY WORKSHOP organized by Dean Wesley Smith and Kristine Katherine Rusch in February 2014. The theme for the anthology was Risk Takers, meaning stories about people taking extreme risks, and it had to involve some sort of game element.

I decided to incorporate the game of cribbage, a game my father taught my brother and I from an early age, and to honor my father's military service with the Canadian Army in World War II where he learned the game.

My father served with the artillery but I decided to use the bomb disposal unit of the Royal Canadian Army Engineers as my subject since they faced incredible risks deactivating and disposing of unexploded ordinance during the war.

What you are about to read is the result of my efforts. And the story that was published in Fiction River Volume 12– Risk Takers in March 2015.

Think of these veterans as you read the story and when the opportunity arises thank them for their service.

In case you're wondering the term Muggins Rules is a unique aspect of the game of crib wherein if a player fails to peg all the points in their hand another player may "steal" them by uttering the term, "Muggins". Check out how this rule applies in this tale of war and sacrifice.

Muggins Rules

LIEUTENANT GUS AIMES CAME TO ATTENTION when Colonel Marks entered the platoon's field tent unannounced. For the first time since the supply company erected the temporary structure to house his platoon, Gus was able to ignore the stale odor permeating the heavy, moldy-smelling canvas. He doubted the Germans would miss such a large tent with their eighty-eight millimeter guns just because the canvas tent was dyed forest green. It seemed a ridiculous precaution but he supposed canary yellow would have been worse.

The colonel had been assigned as Battalion Commander two days before the D-Day jump off so Gus didn't know much about the old man.

The unofficial title of old man for a battalion commander didn't refer to the age of the present occupant of the position; instead it symbolized the respect the men under the colonel's command had for the officer's rank. During wartime a colonel held the power of life and death, so trusting the old man was very important to men on the front lines.

As a bomb disposal platoon, trusting the man next to you, never mind your officers, was critical to morale and a soldier's continued good health.

"Lieutenant." Colonel Marks spoke gruffly then returned the salute with a slight nod of his head. Gus moved to the at-ease position with his hands folded behind his back his legs spread apart.

The colonel scanned the interior of the dimly lit tent, the heavy fabric filtering out most of the sunlight on this very warm day. The stuffy air inside the tent meant the men had difficulty sleeping at night.

"As you were, Lieutenant." Gus dropped his arms to his sides and relaxed the tension in his body. Since when did a lieutenant colonel come to speak personally with a second. lieutenant platoon leader about a mission? In the Canadian Army senior officers barely acknowledged the junior officers' existence.

"Where are your men?" asked the colonel as his searching gray eyes landed on Gus's. "They're out on PT, sir, with Sergeant Carpenter."

One gray streaked eyebrow on the colonel's forehead formed an arch. "Physical training on such a hot day?" He cleared his throat. "Carpenter must be quite the fellow."

"Yes, sir."

The colonel nodded. "Fine. As soon as he returns with the men I want to see you and the sergeant at the Command Post. We have an assignment for you. No later than eleven hundred hours."

Gus glanced at his watch. It was ten thirty hours now. "Yes, sir."

The colonel paused and drew in a sharp breath. He leaned closer to Gus, so close in fact that the odor of the colonel's rum-based aftershave threatened to overwhelm his senses.

4

"It will be a tough assignment. Like none you nor your men have encountered yet. Understood?"

Gus only nodded. As the colonel turned to leave, the heel of Gus's right boot made a snapping sound as it came down hard on the rough pine planks covering the dirt floor of the tent as he came to attention once again.

Before he disappeared out the open tent flap, Colonel Marks locked his dispassionate eyes on Gus again. "Some of you will not survive."

Then he was gone.

Gus's heart rate increased as he stood, paralyzed, unable to breathe for several seconds as the colonel's meaning sunk in. He'd already lost three men since D-Day and there were only seven trained men in his platoon when they set off from England. Writing the letters to the families of the dead tied his guts into knots. Now I'm supposed to lose more of the boys? No. That's not gonna happen.

Finally he let his breath escape his lungs, then bolted for his bunk and snatched his helmet off the rough wool blanket. Slapping the helmet on his head, he exited the tent by sweeping the tent flap aside with one arm, then ran outside.

The compound contained groups of soldiers standing near or seated on shattered tree stumps and fallen logs eating rations, talking in hushed tones, or smoking. He zigzagged

through the groups of war-weary men, some of whom yelled obscenities after him for disturbing their rest period.

He headed for the makeshift exercise field on the other side of camp. He hoped to find Carpenter and his men as quickly as possible.

Time was short.

***

Sergeant Carpenter stood at attention beside Gus in the sweltering heat of the command post tent. Sergeant Carpenter, the oldest man in the platoon at age thirty-one, joined the peacetime militia in 1929 just before the economic collapse brought on the Great Depression. He was a hard man, but a good leader, who refused battlefield commissions when they were offered to him because, while he seemed to enjoy being tough on the men, he also loved being at the center of the action.

In front of them sat the colonel behind the table he used as a desk reading what Gus recognized as one of his action reports. Finally, the colonel set the report on the table and regarded the two men with dispassionate eyes, making Gus uneasy.

"As you were," he said, his tone softer than before, less formal somehow.

Gus relaxed, as did Sergeant Carpenter beside him. "Lieutenant Aimes and Sergeant
Carpenter reporting as ordered, sir."

"Gus, isn't it?" asked the colonel, startling Gus with such an informal address. "Huh, yes, sir."

"I have some bad news for you and the men, and I wanted to tell you personally, Gus."

The colonel paused adding to the growing knot of tension in Gus's stomach. "Captain Williams and First Lieutenant LaPierre were killed early this morning by a sniper. We got the sniper but not before he took out five men including your company commanders."

The colonel stood and walked to the back of the tent where he picked up a pack of cigarettes and a silver-plated lighter off a small table beside his bunk. Walking back to stand behind the table, he offered them each a cigarette, which they both declined. The colonel lit a cigarette then tilted his head back and blew a stream of acrid smoke at the ceiling of the tent.

Avoiding looking at them, he spoke in low tones. "This is very bad timing, Williams and LaPierre were developing plans for a major operation. A plan that involved your platoon of bomb disposal experts."

Now Gus was curious. "In what way, sir?"

The colonel sat down and stubbed the cigarette in a small glass ashtray on one side of the table. He looked up at Gus. "Have you heard of the tall boy bomb?"

Gus and Sergeant Carpenter exchanged a knowing glance. Sergeant Carpenter's brow furrowed. Gus's cheeks became cool and he trembled involuntarily. The tall boy, also known as an earthquake bomb, was dropped by heavy British Lancaster bombers on hardened targets such as bunkers and the heavily fortified installations for the rockets being launched against England.

The Vickers-built munitions weighed twelve thousand pounds and carried enough explosive force to turn a five-story building into pieces of rubble no bigger than six inches by six inches.

The worst part of the bomb for his platoon was many of these particular bombs had time-delayed fuses. The question was when had this bomb been set to go off?

"Huh, yes, sir, we trained on this particular bomb."

The colonel nodded. "Yes, that's in your file. Which is why I need your help." "Help, sir?" Colonels give orders, they don't ask for help, especially from junior Officers.

The colonel's eyes became hard and his brow furrowed. He eased forward in his chair. "There is a tall boy buried in the only supply road to the front not destroyed or mined by the enemy. An operation critical to us winning this war is set for twelve hours from now."

"Can't we just remove the mines from one of the other roads, colonel?"

The colonel shook his head. "Time is against us, I'm afraid. The preparations are complete for the big push. We need that road cleared of the tall boy; it's the only option. Lives are at stake." The colonel handed Gus a folded piece of paper. "These are your orders. Take them to Captain Septon at 4th armored and he'll arrange for transportation."

Assuming the briefing was over Sergeant Carpenter snapped to attention. Hesitating briefly, Gus did the same. They saluted in unison then turned about face and quick stepped out of the command tent.

Once outside, Gus and Sergeant Carpenter shifted to walking, making their way back to the men of the platoon who were busy packing their gear for the assignment. When Gus and Sergeant Carpenter last saw the men, they were in good spirits.

It had been a week since the platoon saw action and the men were growing restless from inactivity. A soldier's greatest enemy was the boredom of war followed by brief spurts of terror and blood.

Gus snorted and stuffed the paper in the breast pocket of his uniform tunic. "Sergeant, you and I have to keep this news from the men as long as possible."

Sergeant Carpenter grunted. "I'm not so sure that's a good idea, sir."

Two soldiers ran in front of Gus and the sergeant, forcing them to stop short to avoid being trampled. One soldier carried a football, the other man chased him. Once Gus and the sergeant could continue walking, Gus said, "Why?"

"Well, sir, a tall boy is a deadly piece of machinery, some of the boys may not make it if the fucker goes off."

Gus chuckled. Sergeant Carpenter was a plainspoken man, but he understood human nature far better than most. "Yeah, sergeant, you may be right. You wanta deliver the bad news or should I?"

As platoon leader, it was technically his responsibility but the sergeant's ability to handle even the most delicate news with the men had pulled his butt out of the fire more than once. Sergeant Carpenter had a gift Gus didn't share.

"I think this time, sir, it should come from you. It's news that's above my pay grade. Sir."

Sergeant Carpenter was right of course; the question was how much did he tell them? The deaths of the captain and the first lieutenant were overshadowed by what was basically a suicide mission ahead of them.

Sure, they had orders but the sudden deaths of McPherson and Reeves two days after landing in France had been gnawing at him and he wasn't sure he could order these men to their deaths.

"OK, sergeant, I agree. I'll tell them about the captain and the lieutenant, but you provide the mission briefing. You know the tall boy bomb better than anyone in the platoon."

Sergeant Carpenter sighed. "Yes, sir, I agree."

The platoon came into view gathered outside the tent. The men shuffled their feet back and forth looking restless smoking, talking, and sharing a laugh.

9

Well, I dodged the bullet for now, thought Gus, until the real work begins.

***

The Kangaroo personnel carrier had enough room for twenty soldiers, their personal weapons and backpacks, but with their bomb defusing gear, and the four members of the platoon, the passenger area of the open armored vehicle felt cramped. The air reeked of oil and diesel fuel.

The powerful diesel motor behind the passenger and crew compartments made talking impossible, something Gus was eternally grateful for.

Converted from a tank, the personnel carrier's suspension didn't provide a smooth ride. Seated with his back against the steel plating, Gus winced every time there was a sharp bump or a pothole to jar his spine. He looked at Sergeant Carpenter who nodded grimly, the sergeant's mouth a thin line.

The sergeant briefed the men with minimal details about the bomb, telling them its code name was tall boy, and their job was to clear a road as quickly as possible. He didn't tell them about the timing fuse or that tampering with the fuse might set the bomb off.

Every man, including Gus, was highly skilled at bomb defusing so any of them could deactivate the weapon in the dark with one hand tied behind their back. An exaggeration but a testament to the training they'd received at the Royal Army Munitions School over the past two years. Only Gus and Sergeant Carpenter had received the specialized training necessary to defuse the tall boy since the Brit instructors didn't expect they'd ever encounter an unexploded one.

As is often the case in war, the British were wrong.

The Canadian contingent had the smallest bomb disposal platoon amongst the allied armies, but Gus liked to think they were the best. No doubt this was the reason given by the Brits for them being selected for this mission.

But every soldier in the Canadian Army knew the British considered the Canadians expendable. Though the 32nd was good at their job, Gus suspected the real reason they were selected was the Brits didn't want to sacrifice any of their own on a mission with such a low chance of success. In fact, he suspected Allied High Command had other plans, and this operation was a diversion. But orders were orders.

My duty is to complete the mission or die trying. Gus scanned the faces of Antony, Allen, and Sergeant Carpenter. They deserved better after all they'd been through in this war, but they had no choice but to follow his orders.

Finally the personnel carrier came to a stop, rocking forward slightly then settling on its tracks as the din from the engine died to a low rumble. The driver turned in his seat.

"Here's where you get off, sir."

"Sergeant Carpenter, corporal." Gus rose to stand the men's eyes on him. "OK, men, lets unload and get this over with as soon as possible."

"Huh, sir?" Blond, blue-eyed Private Allen spoke first. "Yes, Allen?"

"We'd like to play a game of crib to decide who defuses the bomb, if it's all right with you, sir. As usual the winner defuses the bomb, agreed?"

Gus hesitated. Back at camp they played penny-a-point crib most nights to pass the time. In the field, a game of crib deciding who defused a bomb had become a tradition in the platoon. But the sergeant and Gus were the only ones trained to disarm a tall boy bomb, so this might not be such a good idea. Then again, Allen and Antony were gifted men who learned fast.

"OK, Allen, agreed. But only if we do this fast and not delay too long. We have six hours to get this bomb defused so it can be moved off the road." He brought his left arm up to uncover his watch. "The truck will be here in three hours to lift the deactivated bomb from the crater so the bulldozer and work crew coming after the truck can make the road repairs."

Allen's boyish features broke into a wide smile. "No problem, sir."

Allen grabbed a tool case and tossed it over the armored plates on the side of the carrier where it landed in a cloud of dust with a thud.

Two dozen sand bags, two other tool cases, and a pack containing dynamite soon followed. Though the dynamite had been lifted over the side not thrown over like everything else.

Once the equipment they might need was unloaded, Gus ordered the personnel carrier driver to head back up the road and park. He told him to wait for them until they finished. Gus didn't ask the corporal to sweep up the remains if things went wrong, but the driver's look of discomfort spoke volumes. The corporal didn't want to be within a mile of the massive bomb sticking from a crater in the middle road about a hundred yards from where they stood.

After the carrier moved up the road the platoon formed a half circle around Gus awaiting further orders.

"Sergeant, you and Allen round up a few reasonable sized logs to use as chairs and a table for the game. Antony, you breakout the crib board and cards. I'll wait here."

After a chorus of 'yes, sirs' the men went about their assigned tasks while Gus waited in the middle of the road, smoking what he considered his last cigarette. Birds chirped happily from the stands of trees to the left and right sides of the wide dirt road. The air smelled of jasmine and lilac. It was hard to believe a devastating war was happening on such a perfect summer day.

U.S., British, and Canadian army engineers cut the road through the forest when other available routes were plugged by exploded debris, or were mined by retreating German troops. At least this much of Colonel Marks' story appeared to be true.

Soon the men had four good-sized logs set up with a smaller log in the center, and Milo Antony had the board with two sets of pegs made of wooden matchsticks in the starter holes and the cards ready.

Gus took a seat across from Sergeant Carpenter. "So, Sergeant, you and I against Allen and Antony?"

The sergeant grinned. "You bet, sir."

Team play sped up the game, and since time was short their usual round robin tournament style play would take too long, it made sense. They agreed the first player on the winning team to go out would be the one to disarm the bomb.

"Muggins Rules, sir?" asked Antony. Gus looked at Sergeant Carpenter who nodded his agreement.

Muggins Rules, which are optional, dictate any points a player didn't claim during the counting of that player's score could be stolen by any other player by saying, "muggins."

To some it seemed unfair but these rules forced you to become a better, more attentive player.

Gus shrugged. "Sure, Antony, why not?" "Cut for deal, sir?" said Allen.

Gus grinned at Allen and nodded. Allen picked up the deck and shuffled the cards then set the deck back on the log. He then gripped a short stack of cards and held them up. Each man did the same. Sergeant Carpenter had the high card so he would deal first meaning their team had the first crib. Sergeant Carpenter quickly dealt five cards to each man.

Picking up his cards, Gus saw he had two black threes, a six of hearts, a five of diamonds, and a king of spades.

He could get a double run with the pair if a four came up on the cut, but the percentages were against him with this many cards already on the table.

Each man threw one card face down into the crib on the log next to Sergeant Carpenter to form his crib. Gus threw his ace of spades. Allen, seated to Sergeant Carpenter's right, cut the deck allowing Sergeant Carpenter to turn over the cut card. It was an ace of diamonds.

Gus sighed inwardly, but tried to keep his expression neutral. He had to peg yet so he hoped he'd at least score strong.

Since Allen sat to the dealer's right he played first. The card was a nine of hearts.

Gus scrutinized the card carefully then threw down his six. "Fifteen for two," he said as he pegged two points moving one of their two pegs ahead two holes. Glancing at Sergeant Carpenter he saw a twinkle in the sergeant's eyes.

Antony, seated to Gus's left, threw down another six. "Twenty-one for two," Antony said.

14

Allen glared at his partner his teeth grinding.

If Sergeant Carpenter had a face card or a ten, Gus and the sergeant would have another two points. He did, throwing down a queen of hearts. "Thirty-one for two."

In the next two rounds of pegging, the four players exchanged cards and split seven points each. After Gus counted his cards and added Sergeant Carpenter's crib, the two teams ended in a dead heat at nineteen points each. One hundred and one points left to win.

After four more rounds ended with the sergeant and Gus still in a tie with Allen and Antony, each team twelve points away from victory, Gus realized the next round could be decisive. Gus prayed none of the guys had the winning hand before him. But in case they did, he'd made a decision not to let anyone other than himself disarm the bomb regardless of the outcome.

Pegging had been incredibly strategic. Very few points had resulted from pegging to this point in the game.

After Gus was dealt his cards, he picked them up and saw he would be one point short of going out. Two jacks, a five of hearts, three of spades, and a six of clubs. Gus prayed the cut card was good, or he wouldn't have the points necessary to win. Antony, seated to his left, would count last since he had the crib. But if Allen, or Sergeant Carpenter, had a good hand they would knock him out of the game before he could count his score.

After the round of pegging, Gus still needed one point to win. Shit, I'm done.

His fingers trembled as he picked up his cards and waited for the others to play theirs. Sergeant Carpenter had nothing so it was all up to him, and Allen had seven, one short of going out as well. Now the game depended on Antony's two hands.

Gus's heart sank as he placed his cards on the table. "Six," he said.

Antony revealed his cards and he too didn't have enough to go out. Gus's heart raced. He still had a chance.

"Muggins, Lieutenant," said Allen.

Did I miss something? Gus glared at the private. "What do you mean, Mr. Allen?" "You didn't count the jack of the cut up, sir." He pointed at the two of clubs on top of the deck. "You have a jack of clubs in your hand, therefore you have jack of the cut up, which adds one point to your total score." Allen moved his matchstick one hole. "Which

I believe gives me the win."

Gus's heart sank. Allen was correct; he'd made a stupid mistake. Stealing a furtive glance at Carpenter he saw the sergeant's scowl directed at him. He didn't blame the sergeant for being mad; he'd blown it, and might have just cost Pete Allen his life.

Gus jumped to his feet his boots sinking into the soft, dry earth. "No! I'll defuse the bomb."

"But I won, sir," said Allen standing, his eyes reflecting his confusion.

"I don't care. I'm doing the job." Gus strode away toward the stacked equipment cases.

Sergeant Carpenter came up beside him matching him stride for stride. "Sir," began the sergeant, "do you think this is a good idea? The men enjoy these games. The winner always gets the honor of defusing the bomb."

"Not this time." Gus locked his eyes on the equipment cases. He'd grab the portable tool kit and a vest, which was all he'd need. "Order the men to set up the sandbags and then get behind them."

"I'll go with you, sir."

16

Gus stopped and turned to face Sergeant Carpenter. His heart beat rapidly; his hands formed fists. "You'll be with the men behind the sandbags."

"But, sir—"

"That's an order, sergeant!"

"Muggins Rules, sir," said the sergeant from between gritted teeth. His eyes were narrow and a deep frown darkened his features. The air between the two men was charged with electricity.

Gus could see Sergeant Carpenter was serious. "I'm your superior officer, Sergeant Carpenter, stand down or face a court martial." A court martial during wartime for disobeying the orders of a superior drew an automatic death sentence. The sergeant was taking a serious risk by sticking his neck out for the men.

They both knew Gus's threat was an empty one. He loved these men like brothers and had never pulled rank to override the results of a crib game until now. Sergeant Carpenter must have recognized Gus's decision would forever change the relationships within the platoon. The war was far from over, so any damage to the cohesiveness of the men, and their loyalty to each other, would be irrevocably torn apart.

"Muggins Rules, sir," said Sergeant Carpenter again his tone more determined his muscular body stiff with anger.

Gus regarded the sergeant in silence for several seconds searching Carpenter's eyes for any leeway. Seeing none, Gus willed the feeling of frustration at losing the game slowly dissipate. Sergeant Carpenter was right. Gus had to grant the request, but he needed a way to exit gracefully without compromising his position of authority, and save Sergeant Carpenter from a firing squad.

"Are you asking, sergeant?" "Yes, sir, I am."

Sensing the eyes of the men were on them Gus lowered his voice so only Sergeant Carpenter would hear his next words. "Well then, sergeant, you better get the tool kit and a vest and get started. You agree?"

A slow grin spread over Sergeant Carpenter's rugged features. "Yes, sir, I'll get started immediately."

"Carry on, Sergeant," Gus said louder this time so the men could hear him.

***

Gus helped the men stack the sandbags while Sergeant Carpenter retrieved the tool kit and the vest then made his way up the road toward the massive bomb.

After stealing a quick look over the wall of sandbags, Gus saw the sergeant was using a screwdriver to remove the casing near the tail-end of the bomb. That was where the timing fuse would be located.

Gus waved to Allen and Antony to take cover then dropped down behind the sandbags and covered his head with his hands. Gus crunched his body into as tight a ball as possible, closed his eyes and waited for the explosion. Gus knew the tall boys were too sensitive to be safely deactivated. An explosion was imminent.

After what seemed forever, Sergeant Carpenter appeared from one side of the wall of sandbags. Gus wanted to grab him in a bear hug. "Sergeant Carpenter! You're alive!"

Gus, Allen, and Antony leapt to their feet shouting with joy and slapping a grinning

Sergeant Carpenter on his back and shoulders.

Suddenly from overhead a deafening roar that could only be created by powerful aircraft engines interrupted their celebration. They stepped out from behind the sandbags in time to see a flight of three Mosquito fighter bombers, the bomb bay doors on the planes' underbellies already open, burst across the clear sky flying low over the trees from the east side of the road. They were headed in the direction of the trees on the west side.

Within seconds they dropped their bombs into the trees while their four nose-mounted .303 machine guns fired continuously. Their attack run resulted in large explosions sending boiling balls of yellow-and-red fire and smoke high into the sky. Then the echo of the fast planes powerful engines faded as the planes disappeared over the horizon to the west leaving billowing clouds of acrid black smoke in their wake.

"What is that all about?" asked Allen.

"That, my son, is the destruction of a German recon group." "Sir?" said Antony.

Gus shifted his gaze to Sergeant Carpenter. "The tall boy wasn't armed was it?"

"No, sir," said the sergeant cheerily.

Gus laughed and slapped Carpenter hard on the back causing him to stumble but still managing to stay on his feet. "Our operation is a decoy. Command wanted the Germans to think the road was permanently out of action. No doubt the Germans thought even if we failed, and the bomb exploded, the road would be destroyed and their efforts to delay our forces while they regrouped would have succeeded." Gus shook his head. "Those clever bastards at Command."

"And they took out the Germans' recon group so they wouldn't report we disarmed the bomb?" said Antony.

Gus nodded.

"Oh, boy," said Allen, tipping his helmet back on his forehead with one hand. "And they say we take risks."

"Muggins Rules," said Sergeant Carpenter his tone heavy with sarcasm. "Sergeant?" asked Gus, not understanding the crib game reference.

"They stole our glory, sir, when we could have saved the day like we always do." The four men looked at each other, then broke out laughing.

In the distance, the rumble of numerous tracked vehicles headed in their direction from the allied lines confirmed Gus's scenario. Like the games of crib they played, the war would continue, and he and his men would do their best to help the allies.

Sounds That Angels Make

AT FLIGHT SCHOOL MY TRAINING OFFICER TOLD ME that tail gunners seldom survive their second or third missions.

"Nazi fighters *always* go for the tail gunner," he assured me.

I know. I was shot down nine times. But for some reason I only remember the fourth.

That fourth time, I clearly recall the smell of my leather flight jacket, mingled with the oily smell of the freshly greased gun turret. And I remember the banshee's howl of the wind when the last of our four engines coughed and died. Our Wellington bomber was in agony when she pitched over and began her slow spiral downward to her inevitable destruction. Mostly I have no problem recalling the sinking feeling in the pit of my stomach as the airplane seemed to be coming apart around me.

Then there was the lieutenant's toneless voice over my headset, saying, "Abandon the plane—bail out if you can."

I remember Paul—the little guy from Halifax—he saved me that fourth time.

But I can't remember what happened to him.

21

But who is this guy staring at me? He certainly isn't Paul. In fact, he isn't anyone I know or have ever known. Odd thing is, there is a sad look in his hazel eyes as if he knows me.

***

Allan Culbreath squirmed inside as he faced his father. He squirmed every time he visited the Sunshine Care Facility. The air was always too hot and oppressive. It made him sweat. He kept his bomber jacket on during his visits to his eighty-five-year-old father. He kept his jacket on because he wanted to feel like he could bail any time he felt like it. These visits were getting harder and harder to bear. Besides, Dad was never happy to see him anyway.

Abner "Sandy" Culbreath stared quizzically at his son, his brown eyes uncomprehending and his pale face drawn and gray. Sandy was a war hero. The man who every year laid the wreath at the Cenotaph on Remembrance Day. The man with the chest full of medals. The rarest of the few to survive the horrors of war. A great man. At least that's what everyone said.

To Allan, Sandy Culbreath was the boss, the old solider who just couldn't leave the war behind. Sandy was the general who demanded too much of his children and then expected more.

Allan's sister Susan tried to win her father's love by becoming a lawyer, and a dammed good one. She was also the mother of two bright, red-haired twin girls who attended the best private school money could buy. And her husband was a B.C. Supreme Court judge. The perfect nuclear family. She'd made Sandy proud. He always said so at family gatherings.

Allan took another road. He was the rebel. He dropped out of high school in his grade twelve year.

22

He had gone in search of adventure in the logging camps of B.C.'s interior. What he'd found was alcoholism, a couple of divorces, and two kids who didn't know him. Allan was the black sheep, a disappointment to his father.

After Mom died, Sandy lived with Susan and her family until Susan sent him to this care home to die. That's what Allan accused Susan of when she told him their dad had become too much for her to handle.

"How dare you! Just because you're clean and sober for once doesn't mean you can dictate to me!" Susan said furiously when he questioned her decision to place their father in the Sunshine Care Home. "I know what's best for Dad. I've been his sole caregiver up to now, so that trumps any objections you *think* you have. *You* haven't been around."

It was a tough argument to counter since it was true. If only he'd been there for Dad earlier—Allan's regrets were, as usual, too little, too late.

Truth be told, Sandy's advancing Alzheimer's had made looking after him at home impossible. Even if he imagined he could take the old man to live with him, it wouldn't be safe or in Sandy's best interests.

While living with Susan, Sandy had left a stove element on with a newspaper thrown across it and very nearly burned down the house. Another time he had let their Cairn Terrier, Buddy, loose to roam the neighborhood until Susan came home from work. Sandy adamantly denied he had any part in the dog's escape, but a neighbor confirmed she saw him shooing Buddy out the front door earlier that day.

Susan's daughters were frightened by Sandy's sudden outbursts of anger over the smallest of imagined infractions.

The uncontrollable rages were occurring more frequently and with ever increasing intensity.

"No," Susan insisted, "Dad needs professional, twenty-four-hour-a-day supervision."

Allan reluctantly agreed. It was the right thing to do.

"How ya been?" Sandy said suddenly, interrupting his thoughts. One gray eyebrow on the old man's forehead shot upward, while his opposite eye squinted at Allan. Sandy's hands folded over one another in front of him on the plain pine table in the residents' coffee area. A glass of water, drawn from the bottled water dispenser that sat next to the small, white refrigerator against one wall, sat untouched in front of him.

Allan shifted his left butt cheek on the natural pine chair he sat on. He was getting numb bum. "Huh—not too bad—Dad—"

Both of Sandy's eyebrows shot up and his eyes registered his surprise. "Dad?" He shook his head and chuckled, his thin frame shaking.

A gnarled hand, with a large, dark liver spot on pale flesh so thin you could see the blood vessels through it, wrapped around the glass and brought it to his lips. He took a short sip, then placed the glass back on the table.

"But, Dad—"

Sandy's face twisted in anger and his voice was sharp as a dagger when he said, "Stop calling me that! I'm not your father! I'm not anybody's father!"

A nurse's aide, a large, middle-aged woman dressed in the standard issue medical white pantsuit who was busy serving juice, coffee, and tea from a trolley to other residents seated in a lounging area behind them, glanced at Allan. He caught her look of concern but waved her away with one hand and nodded.

The corners of her wide mouth curled in a knowing smile. She looked away as she pushed the trolley toward the next resident.

"Yes, of course, Sandy. Sorry." Just as Doctor Barnes had instructed him, he knew it was best to acquiesce to his father's delusions at this stage of the disease. Contradicting him only upset Sandy unnecessarily, and made conversation more difficult than it had to be. Barnes told him correction only fueled confusion, anger, and resentment.

Sandy's anger visibly subsided. "Besides, I know who you *really* are…" Sandy winked knowingly at him.

Allan smiled and nodded.

"You're an angel."

Well, this is a new one. "An angel? Me?" said Allan. He wanted to laugh but managed to swallow the urge.

Sandy waved one gnarled hand at him as if he were swatting a pesky mosquito. "Of course you are. You're Paul—Halifax—you remember—the fourth time—the sound. *Now* I know what those sounds were—after all these years—" Sandy's cherubic face looked like that of a kid on Christmas morning.

By contrast, Allan's face was a mirthless smile and he nodded again. What was his father talking about? Fourth time…? Paul? Halifax?

"The sound?" he asked at last.

"You are a sly one." Sandy leaned closer to him and winked, startling Allan. Sandy waved for his son to come closer, as if he wanted to share a secret. Allan leaned closer until his father's lips were next to his right ear. Sandy whispered, "The sound of your wings. The sounds angels make."

Pulling back, Allan nodded. "Yeah. My wings. Of course." *Time to bail.*

25

"Well, Sandy, I gotta get goin'…huh…I've got a lotta stuff to do—"

"Yeah, I'm sure you do. You got the work to do for you know who." Sandy pointed one arthritic finger toward the ceiling. He smiled, a look of beatific satisfaction that made Allan feel, surprisingly, happy.

Maybe delusions when your time on Earth was nearing its end weren't so bad. Good thing his Dad didn't think he was the devil.

***

Out of the corner of one eye I saw the figure crawling toward me. Yup, there he was. Working his way toward me, until he stood behind me. Paul. He helped me undo the safety straps that held me in place and then put his hands underneath my armpits to assist me to stand. With my shattered leg, I certainly couldn't stand by myself.

I felt warm blood trickling down my thigh. I couldn't feel the leg, but I knew it was badly damaged. A bullet had shattered bone into my left leg just before the plane died. I wasn't going anywhere… except for Paul…my angel from Halifax…

I placed one arm over his shoulder as Paul took on my weight. Together we made it to the exit hatch. Time was short so we didn't say anything to each other.

The hatch was open and the roar of the air rushing past the badly shot-up fuselage was deafening. Even if we had wanted to say something, we couldn't. The last I saw of Paul was his triumphant expression as he pushed me out the hatch.

Since this night was cloudy, I fell earthward in the inky cold of utter darkness. I couldn't see anything below me.

As soon as I had counted to five, I pulled the ripcord and felt my parachute barreling out of the pack on my back. This was followed by the sharp jerk upward as the chute opened above me.

The pain in my damaged leg exploded. My head felt as if it were swirling in a Sargasso Sea. I knew I was going to black out. Trouble was, I had no idea where I was falling. If I landed in water, I'd drown for sure. If I snagged a tree, I could become tangled in my parachute lines and hang myself. My leg was useless. No help there.

I struggled to keep my eyelids open, but they felt as if they were composed of lead. Colorful spots of white sparkled at the edges of my vision. I knew I was only seconds from passing out.

Just as darkness overwhelmed me, I heard a sound and felt a warm breeze blow over me from behind. It was an odd sound, like that of a bird when it flutters in the trees.

I strained to see against the impenetrable darkness, hoping to catch a glimpse of something, anything. My mind was clouded by pain. My head lolled forward and I was gone.

***

Dr. Barnes eased back in his leather office chair and sighed. In front of him was a well-worn gray file folder. He looked over his reading glasses at Allan Culbreath seated across from him.

The man's ruddy complexion and neatly trimmed goatee, shot through with streaks of grey, made him look older than his fifty-four years. Barnes knew Allan was a recovering alcoholic and hoped his father's death wouldn't send him off the wagon.

"Sorry about your Dad," he said simply.

Allan's reddened eyes betrayed a range of emotions, then he said, in a toneless voice,

"It's okay, doc. He was sick. These things happen to guys his age."

Barnes leaned forward and rested his long arms on his oak desktop, interlacing his fingers. "Yeah, I know, but your Dad, he was something special—a war hero. All those medals…and surviving being shot down nine times—truly a remarkable man, your Dad."

Allan grimaced ever so slightly, then his eyes drifted away to look at the light brown carpet that covered Barnes' office floor. He couldn't say anything.

Barnes nodded. "Yeah—anyway…"

Barnes stood up and buried his hands in his white lab coat. He wore the plain white smocks because they made the doctors identifiable as doctors to the residents.

"You want to get your Dad's things?"

Allan nodded and stood up. Together they entered the gray and white linoleum-lined corridor and started walking toward the residents' rooms. Each room was numbered and there was a picture of the resident on the door so they would know which one was theirs if they got lost.

Nurses and nurses' aides walked by them smiling briefly and professionally, until they stopped outside room number 222. Sandy's unsmiling gray features and sparkling, intelligent eyes stared back at them.

"Do you want me to go in with you?"

Allan avoided Barnes' gaze and shook his head.

Barnes walked away leaving Allan at the door. Sandy Culbreath was a hero and his son was putting on a brave face.

***

Closing the door behind him, Allan was overwhelmed by the antiseptic smells of his father's room and felt his stomach twitch. The single bed had been stripped and the curtains were open, revealing the lush green grass and the stands of fir and oak trees that acted as a barrier to the road beyond. Mounds of rich brown soil were dusted with sprays of red, yellow, and blue flowers of every kind.

Dad must've enjoyed the view, he thought.

He moved to the bed and stared at the naked mattress. He saw a radio alarm clock that Susan's kids bought for their grandfather on his last birthday, resting on the small nightstand. Not that Sandy listened to music. He was tone deaf due to the damage caused by the bomber's engines during the war.

Three photographs in cheap plastic frames hung on the burnt-orange wall over the nightstand. There was one of him and two of Susan, her husband, and the twins.

Sliding the single drawer in the nightstand open, he got a surprise. Lying flat in the drawer was a framed picture of Sandy in his uniform. Standing beside Sandy was a smiling, red-haired man, also dressed in an RCAF uniform. Pulling the picture out, he saw the inscription handwritten in black ink. It read, *To Sandy, from your Halifax angel, Paul.*

Allan's hands began to tremble and his knees turned to gelatin. He stepped back and sat down on the bare mattress.

He stared at the picture of the two comrades-in-arms with their arms wrapped around each other's shoulders, big grins pasted to their faces.

Allan felt warm, salty tears begin to flow from his eyes. Now he knew what his Dad was trying to tell him. Sandy's stories of the war flooded his thoughts.

Allan remembered Uncle Paul, his Dad's savior and best friend, who died last year.

Allan began to sob. Sandy Culbreath had been back to the time when he heard the sounds that angels make.

The Keel Mountain Conspiracy

NERO KING TIGHTENED HIS GRIP on the butts of his twin nickel-plated .45 automatics, his fingers lightly pressing the triggers, the hammers on both guns cocked. The old 1911's were his babies. Darkness enveloped the majority of the warehouse hiding him in the shadows at the edge of two pools of light formed by circular steel light fixtures hung over their heads. The man he'd been looking for sat at a small square card table under the lights. Two armed burly men, stubble covering their wide faces and strong chins, flanked the thin man, their dark, serious eyes watchful.

His heart beat hard in his chest as adrenaline flowed through his system. The best part of any mission involved the final confrontation. He lived for these moments.

After counting to three Nero stepped out from behind a stack of wooden grates where he'd been hiding and brought the pistols to bear on the two heavy set men. Each carried a South African R1 automatic rifle the barrels pointed at the ceiling.

From their casual stance he assumed they obviously hadn't expected a confrontation.

You can call me trouble with a capital T.

The bespectacled, rail thin, bookish type sitting at a card table between the two-armed giants had to be Albert Mint, his assignment. He certainly fit the description given by the client.

"Don't blink, twitch, or breath..." Nero stepped toward them his pistols aimed at their chests. In case these monkeys made any sudden moves he wanted to ensure his bullets struck the largest target area, on these muscular guards largest could be defined as anywhere on their bodies.

The men glared at him their dark eyes following him as he stepped from the shadows and made his way across the open space separating them. One of the men suddenly lowered his gun intending to shoot causing to Nero fire a pistol once. The sound of the gunshot echoed off the walls of the mostly empty warehouse. A spurt of blood bloomed from the center of the big man's chest. His eyes went wide as his grip loosened on his rifle. It dropped to the floor with a rattle.

The gunman fell back landing on the concrete floor with a smack where he lay still.

The other man ignoring his partner's misfortune lowered his weapon in time to be shot in the kneecap. Howling in pain he fell to the floor dropping his gun in the process. The librarian looking guy stayed seated his eyes wide with fear, his pale forehead dotted with beads of perspiration.

Nero smiled to himself. *I love when a plan comes together.*

Nero holstered one of his pistols keeping the other pointed at the man on the floor then moved to kick the rifle from within reach of the wounded man.

He glared at Nero his eyes fierce and hateful, his flushed features bathed in sweat as blood ran between sausage-sized fingers gripping his blown kneecap.

Nero eyed the man carefully. He wouldn't know much, he was muscle. But why would someone send two such men to guard a timid looking man such as Albert? Nero stole a glance at Albert then looked back at the angry guard on the floor. Something about this situation bothered him.

"Who is this man you're chaperoning?" he asked addressing the guard.

"Go to hell," replied the man between gritted teeth.

Nero holstered his remaining gun then pulled a long thin blade from the sleeve in the inside of his right boot. "I have other ways besides killing you to make you talk." He twirled the blade. It gleamed under the dim warehouse light.

The man sneered at him. "She'll do far worse to me than you could ever do."

Nero pointed the tip of the blade at the guard's eye. "Who are we talking about?"

The man grunted. "I'll never tell ya."

Nero squatted quickly bringing his fist into the man's jaw accompanied by the sound of bone crunching bone. The man went limp his arms flopped to his sides. "No, I guess you won't."

Wincing, shaking his hand Nero rose to his feet and stuck the knife back into the sheath in his boot. "His jaw isn't made of sugar, that's for sure."

"Who are you?" said the man seated at the table.

"If you're Albert Mint I'm Nero King. I'm here to rescue you."

33

Albert's pale brow wrinkled and one thin reddish eyebrow rose to form an arch. "Rescue? What are you talking about?"

Still shaking his bruised hand to ease the pain Nero walked to stand over

Mint his tanned slacks shushing in the still, dusty air. "Someone hired me to rescue you."

"Who?"

"A woman named Holly Pepperwidth paid me a tidy sum to find you and bring you to her."

Mint smirked; his features formed a tight smile. His gray-blue eyes narrowed. "Yes, I see. Holly would employ the use of a hired gun."

Nero froze. His gut instinct had been right again. This mission stunk to...

A throwing knife landed in the middle of the card table with a thunk the grip trembling. Ignoring the pain in his hand Nero stepped around the table and grabbed Mint by his shirt collar with one hand while grabbing his left arm with the other. He dragged the slim man to the floor landing beside him on his stomach using the table as a shield. Another knife struck the now empty chair dead center where Mint had been microseconds before.

The dim overhead lights formed small circles of pale yellow light, beyond were inky shadows. Nero rolled onto his side and pulled out one of his '45's. He fired four times in a random pattern hoping to discourage more knife throwing. Hitting anything would be a miracle.

The sharp report of gunfire quickly dissipated followed by the echo of footsteps slapping concrete as the would-be assassin beat a hurried retreat. The footsteps soon faded until at the opposite end of the facility banged into the wall.

34

He holstered his weapon again. "You okay, Mint?"

"Yes, no thanks to you."

"Those two behemoths are bodyguards aren't they?"

"Yes."

Nero rolled onto his back and sighed. This mission had just become far more complicated. *I hate when this happens.*

***

After exiting the warehouse they hurried to the parking lot where Nero had parked his truck, a sky blue armored panel van with extra duty suspension, wide all-weather tires, and a four hundred and ten cubic inch engine that generated over three hundred and fifty horsepower. The windows were bulletproof. Nothing short of a howitzer could penetrate the armored sides or the windows.

The standard automatic transmission had been removed and replaced with a four-speed stick and the optional heavy-duty clutch. Nero wanted to feel the road underneath him when pissed off clients or ex-girlfriends were chasing him.

Unfortunately there had been far too many of both so this truck had saved his neck many times.

Nero had reloaded both pistols with fresh magazines and had them out to sweep the area as they retreated toward the safety of the truck. His heart beat hard in his chest.

Thankfully the parking lot was unlit so at least they weren't completely vulnerable but the moonless night could hide an entire army of assassin's just beyond out of view.

They were in the open with twenty-five yards to reach safety too far for his comfort. *We're sitting ducks in orange sauce out here.* Suddenly gunfire erupted tearing across the pavement toward them sending chips of blacktop flying in all directions.

Whoever was shooting would find the range soon they needed cover fast. Nero's options for cover were limited. Retreat to the warehouse and wait it out, or run the final few feet to the van. *I don't retreat.*

He fired both pistols in the direction he hoped the fire was coming from then holstered one of the '45's. Grabbing Mint by his arm he dragged the skinny man along beside him running for the safety of the truck. Mint screamed something unintelligible at him but the only thing he could hear was the zing of the bullets and his own rapid breathing.

The snap of ricocheting bullets striking the pavement followed them but they made to the van without being hit. With his and Mints backs pressed to the side of the truck Nero pulled out his other gun. He fired two more shots from each gun in the direction of the incoming fire.

As he 'd hoped there was a brief pause. Stepping to the passenger door he yanked the door handle, it open accompanied by the squeal of hinges. *I really have to oil those one of these days.*

Shoving Mint inside Nero slammed the passenger door then turned to face where he thought the incoming fire originated, his guns at the ready. *All I have to do is get to the drivers side and —* A sharp, painful blow to the back of his head sent the world into a swirling blackness darker than the night then everything around him disappeared.

***

Nero's eyes slowly opened but the world was out of focus. His nose detected the familiar scent of candy bars and soda.

*I must be in my van...*a hard bump and a sudden sway to the left causing his side to bump against the armrest confirmed the truck was moving, fast.

Blinking under an assault of daylight he raised one hand to shield his eyes. All he could make out was the Hawaiian hula dancer air freshener stuck to his dash.

Turning his head slightly resulted in a burst of pain creating multicolored spots blurring his vision. His head throbbed. He touched the side of his face and his fingers touched something warm and sticky. Shutting his eyes again he eased his head back against the headrest.

"Crap!"

"It's okay, Mr. King, the pain will pass soon enough," said a man's voice beside him.

Instinctively Nero reached for his pistols his fingers grasping only empty air in his leather holsters. "Where am I?"

"In your van, of course, isn't that where you wished to be?"

I know that voice.

"Doc? Mint? What the hell is going on?"

"You've been wasting time, Mr. King, Holly has to be stopped before it's too late. I don't care for being addressed as *Doc*, but if you must..." The professor shrugged.

The seat beneath Nero shifted to the right then steadied. *I'm dreaming.*

Forcing his eyes open he blinked until his vision finally cleared. Through the fog of pain he saw it was day, the sun well up in the sky meaning it was well after dawn.

He looked to his left to see Mint behind the wheel his eyes intent on the road.

The knuckles of his thin long fingered hands were crimson from gripping the steering wheel too tightly. Nero nose wrinkled. The Doc reeked strong garlic.

"Mint, I'm way behind in this tale so you better fill me in on the details."

Mint grinned. "Yes, of course, you're right." He paused to step hard on the gas pedal then changed lanes as they passed a tanker truck. Nero's eyes went wide when he saw they were headed at a car in the lane ahead. They pulled in front of the eighteen-wheeler with seconds to spare. The other car sped past its bumper missing them by inches.

Glancing in the side view mirror King saw the car's driver flip them the bird. The large transport truck now behind them blew its air horn for several seconds, the driver registering his anger at Mint's recklessness.

Mint ignored them both. "I expect Holly told you I was kidnapped or something like that, correct?"

"She told me you were kidnapped by slavers..." In hindsight, Nero had to admit it sounded a little lame, he should have checked out her story before he accepted her money. But these were lean times and every buck helped pay the bills.

"A respected Professor of Chemical Engineering specializing in weapons applications, kidnapped by slavers? A lot of people out there want my services but slavers would probably be way down the list of those persons who'd kidnap me. Terrorists of course. Professional thieves, maybe. But slavers? No," He grunted his gray eyes flitting to Nero then back to the two-lane highway.

The strip of sun-warmed asphalt was bordered on both sides by open desert. *We must have travelled a long way since last night. I'm definitely not in Kansas anymore.*

They caught up to a moving truck on a slight grade. The trucks trailer blocked the view of the highway ahead, but this didn't deter Mint from steering into the other lane.

A station wagon not more than a hundred yards away racing toward them fast blared its horn, the heavy car fish tailed wildly as the driver slammed on the brakes.

Mint jerked the van back behind the moving truck just as the station wagon went by its tires smoking, the brakes screaming.

The car's driver, a beefy man with a pasty white face, his eyes closed, gripped the steering wheel trying to control the large car, his arms locked for the inevitable crash.

The other passengers in the stricken car were the typical nuclear family, a woman next to the man screaming, tears streaming down her cheeks, and two terrified children sat in the back seat frozen in place with eyes wide open. A large hairy dog hung half way out a side window barking loudly as the car skidded past.

Nero watched the stricken car in the side mirror next to him and was pleased to see the wagon come to a full stop, albeit it was sideways on the highway, behind them.

Turning his attention back to the Doc he said, "Take it easy, I'd rather get where ever we're going in one piece." His head throbbed causing him to wince. The pain reminded him his pieces were badly beat up right now.

"What?"

"Your bad driving, man, you could have killed us and them."

"Who?"

Nero rolled his eyes. *I give up.* "At least tell me where we're going, Doc."

Mint suddenly looked excited. "Holly plans to affix a dispersal device to a Cessna at a remote airstrip not far from here.

One of her minions will fly over Keel Mountain State Park in Alabama two days from now and release an odorless military grade incapacitating agent."

Nero frowned. "A chemical weapon, really? Military grade? A park? She's going to all this trouble to stun some squirrels? And who has minions anymore?"

Professor Mint sighed. "You ask a lot of questions for a man who killed one of my bodyguards and incapacitated the other. All I'll say for now is hundreds of lives, maybe thousands, are at risk if we fail to stop her in time."

As ridiculous as all this sounded Nero decided he better play along, at least until his full facilities returned, and he found his missing .45's. "OK, Doc, sorry. What can I do to help?"

Nero had to make this right. Anger burned in the pit of his stomach at the thought of Holly Pepperwidth tricking him into doing her dirty work. It didn't sit well. She would pay dearly for the life of the man he killed for her and the additional lives she now threatened.

Hold on. "Doc, who knocked me out back there?"

"I did."

***

They drove for several hours until nightfall when Nero pointed out a motel sign just ahead.

After a brief discussion, the professor protesting any stopping would be dangerous saying they had to get to the airstrip as soon as possible. Upon being questioned further Mint admitted he had no idea where to look for Holly and her minions, as he called them. They finally agreed they'd stop for a few hours to get some food and rest so they'd arrive at the airstrip just after sun up the next morning.

Nero explained it might be better to confront Holly in daylight than darkness.

Mint reluctantly agreed this was the best strategy.

After a supper of stale ham sandwiches, from the gas station beside the motel and a cup of cold coffee, Professor Mint explained the chemical agent Holly planned to disperse is called *3-Quinuclidinyl benzilate*, or BZ for short. In it's gaseous state BZ is odorless, colorless and doesn't usually kill. The effects of the agent include stupor, confusion, and confabulation, with concrete and panoramic illusions and hallucinations, and a regression to primitive, involuntary behaviors such as floccillation and disrobing.

Nero listened intently to Professor Mint's explanation, but after he finished nagging questions remained unanswered.

"Doc, Holly's dispersing this gas over a mostly empty state park. Why wouldn't she gas Fort Knox or New York City or Washington D.C.?"

The professor's gray face narrowed as his jaw tightened and his eyes avoided Nero's intent gaze. "She's after the largest lost treasure in United States history."

Nero eased back on the bed causing the worn springs in the mattress to creak. The professor snorted derisively. "I know, I know, Mr. King, I too was skeptical, but Holly found a map that shows where a Confederate Guerilla, Jeremiah McCain, hid two chests of captured Union gold in 1865. She plans to use the gold to fund a private army to take over the country."

"You must be kidding..."

Mint snapped his head toward Nero and locked eyes with him. His mouth formed a grim line and his eyes burned with conviction. "I wish I was, Mr. King. People will die and she will destroy the country as we know it."

Guy's the nutty professor. I better continue playing along to find out what's really going on.

If what Mint said about the plane and the chemical agent was true then he had to do the right thing and at least get to that airstrip before the plane took off. But this gold story had to be pure fiction. *Take over the country? Ridiculous.*

"Well then, Doc, I guess we better get some rest for a couple of hours then head for that airstrip. But first I'll need my pistols. Where did you hide them?"

Mint's face brightened and he grinned. "Sorry, but I had to disarm you so you wouldn't shoot me until I had a chance to explain."

"How did we get away from those gunmen back at the warehouse?"

"I used your guns to drive them off after I knocked you out."

The professor didn't look like a man who knew much about firearms but in Nero's experience looks could be deceiving. "Good for you, Doc, but where are they?"

"Under the passenger seat of the van."

Feeling stronger after eating and drinking Nero rose to his feet and since he'd taken off his boots after entering the motel room he slipped them on his black as Mint handed him the keys for the van. After smoothing his black pants and matching sweater with the palms of his hands he walked to the door.

Once outside he made his way to the truck parked across the lot from the room barely visible in the dim light cast by the neon road sign next to the highway. Stands of pine trees bordered the motel on three sides. There weren't any stars visible meaning it was cloudy, the weather had changed since they started this mad dash.

Curious, why didn't he park in front of the room? After unlocking the driver's door he opened it and climbed inside.

42

He'd disabled the interior light when he modified the van so he sat shrouded in darkness. For the first time since this mission began Nero was alone with his own thoughts. He let out a long breath and his body sagged like a balloon with a slow leak.

A sudden movement near the trees to his left made him freeze. I must be imagining things. A brief glint of light confirmed something was moving near the trees.

Suddenly three figures dressed in black fatigues, protected by Kevlar vests, their faces hidden by balaclavas and night vision goggles, moved quickly from the cover of the trees into lighted parking lot.

They moved with military precision to set up a field of fire on the motel room shared by him and the professor. They were armed with HK MP5's and the butt of a pistol stuck from a chest holster on each shooter.

These were professionals, not the ragtag force he had expected to find if even half of the Doc's story was correct. The professor's wild tale might be not so wild after all. Holly could be a much greater threat than he first thought.

The familiar burn of excitement prior to imminent action rose form deep inside him. Nero leaned forward and quickly found his pistols under the seat where the Doc said he stashed them.

Checking the magazines he confirmed they were fully loaded. Now it didn't fit what the Doc had said about driving off the gunmen. If they were pros like these obviously were.

Pressing a recessed forest green button on the dashboard flipped open a hidden compartment revealing three rows of extra magazines for his guns and six hand grenades. He pulled four magazines and three grenades from the supply and put them on his weapons belt attached to his twin holsters.

He expected if he managed to surprise these goons he'd need the extra ammunition and the grenades. If not then this could well be his last day among the living.

Holstering one gun, he swung the van door open slowly so as to minimize any noise. Leaving the door open and extracting his second pistol he bent low. He moved as quietly as possible as he made his way around the van. Swiftly he crossed the lot until he was behind the trip of gunmen. He stopped, aimed at the gunmen at the opposite ends of the parking lot; the one in the middle was probably the leader. Nero wanted him alive to question him.

"Excuse me," he said loudly.

The three shooters froze for a fraction of a second then the ones at either end spun around trying to turn their guns on him. Nero fired twice, the sound echoing off the motel walls.

The two gunmen dropped as if they were puppets whose strings were suddenly cut. Blood flowed from the head wounds where the bullets entered scrambling their brains.

The remaining gunman dropped his MP5 and raised his hands above his head. "Don't shoot," said a feminine voice.

A woman? "Drop to your knees and lock your hands behind your head." She did as instructed. Nero holstered his left pistol and moved cautiously toward her still aiming for the back of her head in case she tried anything. He kicked the three dropped MP5's from her reach then pulled the pistol from her holster. After tossing it aside he stepped back.

The door to his motel room burst open and Professor Mint rushed outside. "What's going on out here, Mr. King? It sounds like a shooting gallery." Mint pulled up and stopped his gaze drifted between the two dead men finally stopping to stare at the woman on her knees.

"Who is that?" he asked, his tone angry his brow wrinkled. His gray pallor grew darker.

"Let's see," Nero replied then moved to stand over the woman. He yanked off the balaclava revealing an emerald-eyed woman with red hair shot through with wine colored streaks. She glared at him, contempt in her eyes.

"Holly?" said the professor, his demeanor changing instantly to fear.

Now Nero was really confused. "So, Doc, you're telling me this is Holly Pepperwidth?" The professor nodded his eyes still fixed on the woman. "OK, now this is getting beyond ridiculous. You're telling me the woman who tried to kidnap you, hired all these gunmen trying to kill us, is planning to take over the country is this woman? Is that what you're telling me?" By now Nero was shouting.

"Yes, yes, Mr. King," The professor replied waving him away as if he were a pesky fly. "And she's my daughter so please don't hurt her." To emphasize his point Professor Mint pulled a Beretta 9 mm automatic from the small of his back and pointed it at him. "And kindly drop your weapons before I am forced to shoot you."

Nero stared uncomprehendingly at the chemical weapons specialist. "Do it now, Mr. King." Nero loosened his grip on the '45's and they fell to the pavement with a rattle. "Kick them away." Nero did this.

Holly stood then moved to stand beside her father. "Tell him to toss me the grenades on his belt." Glaring at Nero her expression suggested her absolute contempt for him.

This was the lowest point in his life. It weighed heavily on his shoulders.

The professor and his nut bar daughter had fooled him completely.

"And don't try any funny business. Pulling a pin will be rewarded by a bullet between the eyes." She spat the words as if they tasted like vinegar.

Nero acknowledged his defeat with a sigh. He tossed her the grenades one at a time. "Now what?"

Mint glanced at his daughter then back to him. "We head for the airstrip and the plane."

"You two are planning to over throw the government are you?"

Holly uttered a harsh laugh. "Of course not. Who would believe such crap?"

Nero held back a wince. *Ouch, that hurt.* "You plan to keep the gold, correct?"

She nodded, the bitter smile on her face eased slightly. "And these guys." He nodded at the dead gunmen sprawled across the parking lot. "They're survivalists or some such who believed your story about taking over the country with the gold. Correct?"

The remainder of her smile was replaced with a scowl. "Father, take this man out behind the motel and get rid of him. He's a loose end."

Pulling a tactical knife from the sheath on her hip she walked up to him. For a second he wondered she would do the deed herself, but she held the knife to his throat as she patted his pockets until she found the van's keys. After relieving him of them she spat in his face. "You've interfered with my plan for the last time, King," she then headed for the van

Warm spittle ran down his face as Professor Mint urged him forward with one of the MP5's he had retrieved from a dead gunman. When they were out of sight of the parking lot Nero said, "She's crazy you know, Doc."

46

"Watch what you say or your time will end sooner than planned."

"OK, OK, sorry. She did actually hire me to rescue you didn't she? What's bothering me is who kidnapped you? The only culprits I can come up are some of her survivalist buddies."

"Why would she do that?"

"I think she hoped they'd kill you and keep then she could keep the gold for herself."

They stopped and Nero could see Mint considering his words pasted across his features. "That doesn't make sense, King, she needs me."

"For what? She has the chemical agent, the dispersal device, and she has the map. So my question to you is what purpose do you serve now?"

The doubt on Mint's face was evident. He lowered the barrel of the gun, his eyes drifting away from him. Now would be his only chance. Nero delivered a perfectly targeted and executed roundhouse kick to the gun in the professor's hands. The gun flew away landing over twenty feet away.

"Why you..." Mint charged him his features twisted by anger.

Nero sidestepped the professor, his momentum carried him forward passing Nero on his left. As he went by Nero locked his hands together and brought them down like a hammer on the back of Mint's neck. The older man collapsed in a heap at his feet.

Kneeling beside the unconscious man Nero checked for a pulse and found it was there although weak. *He might make it, but I have to stop her first.*

He grabbed the MP5 from the dirt and ran around the buildings.

After ensuring the gun was on single shot he took aim at the van and let loose with a single shot. The bullet snapped off the protective windshield next to where Holly stood behind the armored door awaiting the return of her father.

Screaming something he couldn't make out, his heart pounded in his chest when she raised grenades and threw it at him. Dropping to the ground he rolled to his left hoping the grenade had been tossed in the opposite direction. He gritted his teeth as it exploded a few yards away, his cheek was torn by a shard of shrapnel. Pain seared through him. He tasted blood on his lips.

Jumping to his feet he ran headlong at her firing repeatedly. He watched as she pulled the pin on another grenade. He halted, aimed at the door, and fired three shots in quick succession. Instinctively she scrambled into the van the door closing it behind her still holding the now live grenade.

Her eyes went wide when she realized her error, but it was too late. The grenade exploded the shrapnel shredding flesh, vinyl, and the Hawaiian hula dancer air freshener on the dashboard. The concussion from the force of the explosion punched out the windows. Smoke poured from all areas of the vehicle.

Breathing hard, Nero lowered the gun suddenly weary and stared at his wrecked van.

"Well, I guess I'm not going to be paid for this job."

A nervous looking motel clerk, with big eyes and glasses, appeared from the office. "Hey, mister, what's going on out there?"

"Call 911," he shouted back.

The skinny bespectacled man nodded and disappeared back into the office. *I'm gonna let the law enforcement guys figure this mess out.*

48

One thing he knew for sure was Holly intended to fly the plane herself. She didn't want to share the money with anyone, and she'd kill to do so, even her father. He smirked to himself and lowered the gun to his side. Greed is a terrible curse.

Lost Stories

The Martians, encased in their gray metallic hulls, the long, accordion-like legs of their monstrous machines crushing everything in their path, strode across the green hills, rushing toward me.

The alien monsters' hundred-yard-long spider-like legs and tremendous weight caused the ground beneath my feet to tremble with each terrible footfall, as if wracked by a force nine earthquake.

With a super-human feat of insurmountable strength, I managed to remain standing on the shaking and roiling ground as rivulets of sweat trickled down my forehead.

The Martian heat rays transformed everything they touched into red and yellow flames. Buildings, and even people, became candles of leaping fire as they were caressed by the lights of death.

From my perch on the hill overlooking the once green expanse of valley now turned to smoke, I watched in horror as the machines destroy my world. Acrid smoke from the burning landscape invaded my nostrils and mouth.

As I witnessed the growing destruction, I knew deep in my soul that I had to stop these invaders from another world before humanity was a distant memory. The world needed a hero and I, Elmer Johnson, knew I had to be that hero.

***

"I'll stop them!" Elmer's raucous but raspy voice echoed through the narrow corridors of the Sunny Vale Rest Home.

Jane Peters eased back into the padded lime green leather recliner and sighed. Every bone in her lean body ached from the effort of getting him seated in his chair. How he'd gotten loose again she could never figure out.

Elmer's delusions were definitely getting worse. The old man's gnarled hands extended outward from his ravaged, emaciated frame, as if his bony limbs allowed him to soar above his wheelchair like some large-winged seagull, looping and swooping in an invisible aerial dance. Elmer's gray eyes glowed with an intensity reserved for young children playing their favorite games.

The pretty raven-haired nurse leaned forward and placed one thin, porcelain hand on Elmer's leathery wrist. The rubber-covered steel wheels of the wheelchair squeaked when he pressed his weight against the seat belt, trying to get up but failing. The chair's wheels were also locked so it wouldn't move.

Of late, Elmer had adopted the habit of pushing the chair around the nursing home, shouting and rambling wildly about fighting monsters from space, or visiting strange planets, or some such other nonsense.

Jane, as director of patient care, had decided he should be moved into the extended-care wing with the other Alzheimer's patients.

Elmer required the calmness of the extended-care environment and the additional medications that the doctor who visited the Alzheimer's ward would prescribe for him.

Jane glanced at the clock over the picture window on the wall that faced the central garden. Mr. Johnson's son, Bert, would be here in the next few minutes.

She needed to deliver Elmer to the alcove, a peaceful sitting area with three worn leather recliners, a few faux wood coffee tables scattered around the space, and an assortment of various chairs of all styles and eras collected over the past forty years.

One wall of the alcove was taken up by a large window overlooking the green valley of trees, bushes, and wildflowers that ran to the horizon.

The low lighting in the room made it a favorite for residents and staff who wanted to have a peaceful moment alone, either by themselves or with family visitors in the case of residents. Not that there were many of those for some of the old dears.

Bert Johnson was different. He showed up every week like clockwork. In fact, Jane had taken to setting her watch by his arrival.

Nevertheless, she would stay with Elmer and hold his hand until Bert arrived.

In her mind she recalled the tall, lean man with the dark hair slightly gray at the temples that flashed through her mind's eye. He'd lost his wife recently to cancer, so this would be a difficult meeting. Her own recent divorce almost made them bunk mates. She blushed as she realized how inappropriate that thought was.

"I've activated the rocket pack. We'll be there as soon as we're able," said Elmer excitedly, straining against the seat belt restraining him from standing. He made rocket engine sounds as if he were once again a child, playing. Jane smiled to herself.

In some ways she envied Elmer Johnson. He was living his early years over. Her heart was heavy when she thought about the aspects of her life where she'd like to have made some changes, if she'd had the chance.

***

The giant, superintelligent termites of the imperial guard marched in formation toward our bristling defenses of laser cannons, shockguns, and heavily armored drones.

As Grand General of the Colonial Army, Elmer Johnson's job was to lead the remnants of the colonial forces in the final battle to purge the galaxy of a horrific, marauding enemy.

The evil warlord of the enemy forces, Garth the Terrible, must be destroyed if peace were ever to be restored to the galaxy. This climactic battle would decide the fate of the universe for millennia, and he wouldn't let them down.

He couldn't fail when he had his voluptuous girlfriend, Becky Ultimate, and his best friend, Sparks McElroy, at his side.

***

She watched with arms crossed over her chest, unable to push herself to interfere. What was so bad about a ninety-three-year-old man re-living his childhood? For all she knew, Elmer Johnson had been a pilot before his retirement. She realized with a burning shame she knew so little about him.

"Look out!" Elmer cried as he threw his hands over his head and cowered, scrunching his body down into the cushioned seat of the wheelchair.

He trembled, buried his face in his arthritic hands, and began to be wracked by deep sobs.

She rushed to his side and wrapped her arms around him in order to comfort him. "It's okay, Mr. Johnson. What's wrong?"

"They're coming to git me!" His voice shook with terror.

"I don't think so, Dad," said a deep male voice from behind her.

Jane let go of Elmer to look behind her and saw Bert Johnson in a red-and-blue plaid work shirt, blue jeans, and white, unsoiled Nike's, with a sly grin on his lips.

Jane's heart beat faster and she had to lick her dry lips. It seemed even the sunlight streaming through the window fell over Bert as if it were a spotlight from heaven itself. His sparkling hazel eyes and strong chin gave him the appearance of a male model on the cover of a romance novel.

She often wondered what he thought of her. A short, middle-aged woman with dyed auburn hair was no catch for a guy who looked like him. How could he possibly be romantically interested in her? Though she did have a decent figure and people told her she had a pleasant face.

Bert moved forward to place one large, calloused hand on his father's right shoulder. For a moment she wondered what he did for a living with those calloused hands, then dismissed the thought as none of her business.

"No one's going to hurt you, old fella. Especially not this nice lady," Bert said as he flashed a row of white teeth at her.

Jane grinned weakly. She felt silly and awkward in front of him, cursing herself for sounding like some silly schoolgirl.

"How's he doin'?" Bert's face changed to a serious expression.

"Not good, I'm afraid," said Jane.

"What do you mean?" Elmer asked, his voice tinged with anger.

He now sat ramrod straight in his wheelchair, glaring at Jane. "An' who the fuck is this guy?" He nodded toward Bert." You fuckin' him?"

Jane's face grew warm and knew she was blushing.

Bert grimaced.

"Perhaps we should step over here," Jane suggested to Bert, indicating the hallway outside the alcove with a slight nod of her head.

They would be out of Elmer's hearing when they moved behind the pale peach wall.

Bert nodded and followed her out until they were hidden from his father behind the wall.

"I'm a space man!"

They were able to still hear Elmer's shout as he returned to his happy persona, emitting sounds of rocket take-offs and ray gun blasts. His maniacal, childish giggles echoed in the hallway.

When they'd moved far enough down the hall so they could speak comfortably, Bert stopped and turned to face her. His eyes seemed to pierce her soul and she had to concentrate to keep her emotions off her face. Her ex-husband always said she wore her emotions on her sleeve. But he was an ass of the first order, so what did his opinion matter?

As they talked, nurses and housekeeping staff moved up and down the well-lit hallway. Their flat, white, nursing shoes made small squeaks as they hurried to their destinations. Their eyes flitted toward Jane and Bert as they passed. Jane could see the look in some of them as they slid off her to Bert. He was really a head turner of a man.

"When are you moving him?" asked Bert, getting immediately down to the business at hand.

"I'd like to do it today, if that's okay."

His gaze dropped to the floor. "Yeah, I guess that would be best."

"We're going to have to drug him. Do you have a problem with that?"

"Why?"

"You heard him," she said, nodding her head toward the entrance to the alcove.

Bert nodded and his shoulders visibly relaxed.

Jane realized up to that moment he must've been ready for an argument. It hadn't occurred to her Bert might object to his father's move, having seen Elmer's condition deteriorate before his eyes these past few months.

"I have the forms in my office if you'll follow me."

Together they walked down the hall past the residents' closed doors until they reached her office. On each door there was a picture of the occupant and their name, written with a felt pen in large black letters on a small whiteboard affixed to the door. The signs were designed to help residents find their rooms when they lost their way.

The sign on her office door held her name and title only, no picture.

Jane's office door swung silently open and Bert followed her inside. Her office window gazed out over the gardens. Sunlight streamed in to give the room a glow. Her dark-stained teak desk was clear of papers, with a plain gray blotter and a black telephone with a string of buttons at the bottom for various incoming lines; her brown leather executive chair sat behind the desk like a solider waiting for her return.

On both walls, oak-stained bookcases ran the length of the room containing countless volumes of medical books.

In front of the desk were two low back wood-framed chairs with brown cushions matching the color of her chair.

She moved around the desk and sat in the leather chair. After opening the drawer on one side, she searched for and found the forms she needed. She had completed them to the point where he had only to sign them, then his father would be placed in the extended-care patient wing.

She placed them flat on the desk, her hands framing them. From a two-pen holder at the front of the desk, she pulled out a blue ballpoint and placed it next to the forms.

"You need to sign where I've marked the X," she said, pointing to the appropriate signature box.

Bert studied the form carefully.

"What does my dad talk about?" he asked, his attention focused on the forms.

"I'm not sure what you mean."

"Does he tell stories?"

She stopped and thought for a moment. "I don't really know." She shrugged. "I could ask one of the staff. Why?"

He paused. "Dad loved to read all his life, and since he moved in here he's stopped reading altogether."

"I'm afraid that's pretty common with Alzheimer's patients, Mr. Johnson. They can't remember each page as they read so they're unable to follow a story from beginning to end. Patients with this affliction are often unable to recall key plot points in stories long enough in their minds to build a cohesive story. This frustrates them terribly, so much so that even life-long readers often stop reading altogether."

"Does Dad have books in his room?"

"Yes, I seem to recall he does."

"May I see them before I sign?"

"Of course."

After leaving her office, they walked down the hall to the room with Elmer's name and picture on the door. Number twenty-six.

Once inside, Bert scanned the room and saw the small wooden dresser, though the matching bedside nightstand was empty. The bed was neatly made, with nice hospital corners, and the room smelled of the antiseptic cleaner common to medical facilities.

Pictures of Bert, and other people Jane didn't know, adorned a small bulletin board next the bed, a reflection of happier times. There were no books. She realized the nursing staff must've removed them.

He nodded and his hazel eyes misted over.

They returned to her office.

"Dad loved his stories," said Bert, his voice edged with sadness. "He's lost them."

After he'd signed, she accompanied him to the front door and keyed the number pad to let Bert out. The key pad was a special security measure so residents couldn't wander, which they tended to try sometimes.

Before they parted, Bert took Jane's hand in his and shook it warmly. She suggested dinner at her place to discuss his Dad's condition. He was surprisingly gentle. As their hands touched, she felt his strength and warmth pass into her body. Her heart nearly skipped a beat when he agreed to meet her for dinner the next day .

The next day Elmer Johnson was medicated and moved to the extended-care wing with the other Alzheimer's and dementia patients.

He was silent and had the glassy-eyed look common to the patients in this wing of the facility. He no longer played or acted like the child his mind said he was.

He looked older now and Jane felt her heart tug as she watched the intern wheel him into the day room where the other patients sat staring unblinkingly at each other, each lost in their own silent worlds of imagination.

Jane blinked the moisture from the corners of her eyes and went to make sure Elmer's belongings were out of his room.

When she arrived, the door was ajar and his picture had been removed. His name had been wiped from the white board.

She went inside and looked round at the now bare mattress and the empty furniture. His clothes were gone and the family photos that had adorned the walls had been removed. She moved to the dresser and opened one drawer.

Inside was a small stack of yellowed magazines with faded covers.

Picking a couple off the top, she read the mastheads: *Amazing Stories* and *Air Wonder Stories*.

The cover of *Amazing Stories* depicted saucer-shaped robots standing on steel stilts with spider-like appendages sticking out from the oval-shaped torso to grasp terrified human figures and lift them into the air. Other long arms of the machines held weapons emitting beams of light that, when they touched shattered buildings, caused the buildings to catch fire.

From the appearance and condition of these magazines, she knew they were very old.

She thought back to what Elmer Johnson had been rambling about in his delusional state of mind. It occurred to her that maybe he hadn't lost his stories after all. Maybe he was living them all over again. She smiled. Bert would be pleased when she told him all about it over dinner at her place.

***

The Martian machines lay in heaps of twisted wreckage as far as the eye could see. Elmer stood with blast rifle cradled inside one well-muscled arm. A light breeze caused his blond curls to ripple like wheat on the prairie and his black-and-gray uniform tunic flapped in the breeze. His calf length, polished leather boots may be scuffed but not his spirit.

He had witnessed the war machines' destruction and his chest swelled with pride at having put up the best defense he knew how.

The evil warlord Garth the Terrible's storm troopers would think twice about attacking the Earth again.

Now we would take the fight to them. And he would lead to ensure victory—victory for Colonial forces and for the galaxy.

Elmer Johnson the alien fighter had been born!

A Shattered Man

Summer. 1971. Seattle.

I STOLE A QUICK LOOK OVER THE DUSTY WINDOWSILL to survey the street three stories below the apartment. Through the dirt-smudged window, I saw that the street was devoid of my neighbors or the enemy. My breathing came in sharp intakes as adrenaline raced through my lean frame, causing the earthy aroma of the sand in the bags I'd piled up along the walls to invade my nostrils.

There were rusting Chevys and Fords parked down both sides of the cracked, blacktopped street, their windows dark. It was a cloudy evening. The streetlights had burned out long ago so the street was blanketed by the inky night. Police cars that had been gathered on the street like angry fireflies earlier in the standoff, bathing the mostly deserted buildings with their flashing red lights, were also gone.

But I knew the pigs were still there, waiting. Waiting for me to pop my head out so their snipers could splatter my brains over the apartment's plaster walls in this fifty-year-old brick walkup.

They'd tried to get to me for the past five hours and paid the price for their overconfidence.

Two dead pigs lay sprawled in their own blood in the hallway on the other side of the steel door I had installed only a week ago. The booby traps I'd laid for them worked as expected. One thing the Viet Cong were good at was building the better mousetrap. It was a lesson the marines had learned the hard way. And a lesson I learned well.

Besides the cops were asshole collaborators. Wally had agreed when he arranged for this apartment for me and introduced me to the gun dealer who sold me the sniper rifle. Thankfully, the dealer'd had a weapon exactly like the one I'd had in 'Nam.

I smiled to myself. I was too good for them. Too well trained.

Dropping below the sill, I padded across the squeaky, bare oak planks. My cotton socks made no sound in the still, humid air. I reached the three-drawer pine dresser where I'd left the M21 rifle.

The rifle sat on the dresser's scarred top at an angle, resting on its polished walnut stock. The matte black stainless steel barrel was elevated, resting on the tripod attached under the barrel ahead of the forestock grip. I'd pulled the dresser away from the wall so I could stand behind it, using the top to rest against to steady my aim. I would choose my targets when they appeared in the windows of the apartment building across the narrow street.

I hadn't heard any movement or seen anyone for more than an hour, but I knew they were planning something. The VC had been crafty bastards too, but we had stopped them. We busted their asses. When the VC attacked our firebase *en masse*, we zapped hundreds of 'em as if they were cockroaches until the survivors disappeared into their tunnels. The VC were more vermin than human.

Sometimes at night when sleep wouldn't take me, I could still smell the bloodied corpses of our dead and the VC dead rotting in the tropical heat—truth be told, most of my nights were sleepless since returning to the world a year ago.

The Seattle cops were no different than the VC. They hid like scared rabbits when I zapped a few of them, too.

I picked at the remains of the roast beef sub I had set next to the rifle and stuffed the chunks of dry bread and grilled beef, coated in tangy barbecue sauce, into my mouth. The tang of the barbecue sauce livened my taste buds. The Blue Diner still made the best subs in Seattle. I had lost thirty pounds during my tour in 'Nam, but the Seattle diet had helped me to regain some of the loss.

The telephone sitting on the small table near the sagging single bed rang loudly, startling me. I reached for the gun, my index finger slipping over the warm steel trigger. My heart raced. I sucked in a breath to steady myself, then pressed my right eye into the eyepiece of the starlight scope affixed to the top of the rifle. I pivoted the gun right, then left, aiming at the windows across the street. The nightscope is able to amplify any light source, even a weak one, allowing the shooter to pierce the darkness. Even starlight would improve the ability to see targets at night, hence the name.

Nothing. No cops. No VC. No civilians.

Slowly exhaling, I pulled away from the eyepiece, lowering the stock again onto the dresser top. I shook my head to clear my thoughts, hoping to ease the pounding headache threatening to split my skull wide open.

I was unable to ignore the telephone's sharp rings any longer. Pain lanced through my brain causing me to wince, my teeth grinding. Persistent pricks.

Son of a bitch. Who's calling? Was it Beth? No. It couldn't be. She said she never wanted to see me again when she stole my kids and left for California.

Bitch. I'll kill her ass after I'm done in Seattle.

I crouched low and rushed to the phone, then lifted the mint-green plastic receiver from the cradle. Thankfully this cut off the ringing immediately, easing the shooting pains across my forehead.

Raising the receiver to my ear, I listened before I spoke. There was a soft click. Bastards were bugging the line. Cops are devils. I'd seen them on TV, smashing heads with batons, shooting demonstrators—kids, really—protesting the war. I hated the pigs.

"Who is this?" I asked, my voice harsh.

The heated air in the apartment had dried out my throat. I needed a drink.

"This is Captain Liam Reilly of the Seattle PD. We have you surrounded, Johnny, me lad. Now be a good boy and come outta there. I promise we won't shoot if you come out without the rifle."

I snorted derisively. "You think I believe you? Really? You're gonna zap my ass as soon I'm in the crosshairs of your sniper's scope. I'm a sniper too, ya know, so I know how it works." I laughed bitterly.

"You a vet?" asked the Captain.

My eyes narrowed and I stiffened. Had they been checking on me? "You guys been talkin' to Beth?"

"Who's Beth?"

I considered the Captain's words for several seconds. My guts tightened and my empty hand formed a fist as my grip tightened around the receiver. "You're stallin' me." I slammed the received in the cradle. Perspiration trickled down my sides under my sleeveless tee shirt with the New York Yankees logo emblazoned across the front.

My mind raced as I sought to understand why the Cap'n had tried to stall me. I finally settled on another attempted assault. Were they complete morons?

I had already killed three, the two in the hall with my booby traps, the third with my sniper rifle during the first few moments of the standoff.

Surely I'd made it clear they were to leave me alone. Did more cops have to die before they understood I was serious? I didn't enjoy killing, but wouldn't shy away from doing so to meet my goals. I'd already zapped the chairman of the local draft board and three others on the board, the so-called upstanding citizens who decided the fates of thousands of my neighbors. Unlike the poor bastards who were being drafted, we'd chosen to fight for our country. I often wondered what was worse: being drafted or volunteering to be tossed into the meat grinder. How could we have been so stupid to volunteer?

Regardless of how anyone ended up in 'Nam, the bleeding had to be stopped. I intended to kill as many people as it took to force them to bring the guys home. The war could not be won. After two tours, I knew this to be true. Death bred death, and I would be the catalyst to change the way things were. I was on a mission to save lives.

Those in power had contributed to the murders of my friends, Spotter and Razorman, who'd died during the defense of our firebase. I had passed judgment on the men who held the power of life and death over our heads as if we were puppets. They deserved to die so lives could be saved and no more boys would be sent to die in that terrible jungle.

The phone rang again. I considered not answering but finally decided I should assess their intention. *Know thy enemy.*

"Hello?" I said, after picking up the receiver.

"Johnny. It's Wally."

Wally Boxer calling *me?* I knew Wally through Billy O'Sullivan's son, Patrick—all us guys in the neighborhood called him Paddy—who I shipped out with to Vietnam.

We'd volunteered for the marines after a wicked night of beers. We were gonna kick some yellow asses. We were convinced the VC would surrender when they heard two Southie boys had joined the fight. "Wally? What's happenin'?"

"Johnny, you gotta surrender."

I couldn't believe my ears. Surrender? Didn't he understand what was a stake? The lives I could save. This was my last stand.

The bastards must be holding a gun to his head, forcing him to trick me. Damn pigs had grown desperate to stop me. I decided to play along. "Sure, Wally. Sure. When do you think?"

"As soon as possible, kid." Wally always called me kid. Not that this was surprising, given he was twenty years older than me and he was an important man in the neighborhood.

Wally had told me and Paddy to volunteer for 'Nam, promising us jobs when we returned. He said the skills we learned in the marines would be an asset to him when we got back.

A grenade trap when on a patrol killed poor Paddy two months into our deployment.

When I returned home, Wally made me a runner for his gang, collecting payments from local businesses who owed him money.

Most shop owners paid willingly every month, but a few either refused or asked for extensions. I made it clear to them they should pay their bills on time. A few broken bones and making the necessary threats against their families emphasized how serious I was about my job. Wally was pleased with my efforts and frequently called me one of his boys. He wouldn't turn on me now. No way.

"Huh. Okay, Wally, how's about when the sun comes up?"

There was a pause at the other end of the line and for a moment I wondered if he'd hung up. Finally he said, "Why sunup?"

"I want the cops to see I'm unarmed. No need in making them nervous. You know how good I am with a gun."

Wally snorted. "Yeah, kid. For sure. I'll let 'em know. And, kid?"

"Yeah?"

"You done good."

I smiled to myself, then hung up. I dropped onto the floor landing on my butt and my shoulders sagged. I hung my head and sighed. The fatigue and stress had caught up with me. I was tired, weary of the war. My war against those in power may have made its point. Maybe I should surrender. Wally might be right.

A day in court explaining my reasons for killing, my need to stop an unjust war. The public had a right to know the truth. My sacrifice of a life behind bars would be worth it if it meant saving a lot of lives.

My body tensed when I heard footsteps across the floor of the apartment above me. The cops were back.

They were planning something after all.

They must have threatened Wally to stall me so they could buy time to position themselves to kill me.

They desperately wanted to guarantee my silence.

They weren't going to let me live to testify in open court.

No way.

A knot of burning anger formed in the pit of my stomach. My hands formed into fists and my head began to pound, shooting pains across my tortured brain.

Ignoring the pain, I dropped onto my hands and knees and crawled to the dresser. Once there, I stood and lifted the rifle until it rested on the tripod attached to the forestock. I pulled the magazine and verified there were still eight cartridges remaining. One more would be in the receiving chamber.

There were sixteen more magazines in the top drawer of the dresser and six extra boxes of ammunition.

A thud overhead startled me. Shoving the magazine back into the weapon, my grip tightened on the trigger and the forestock, my fingers slick with sweat. I swung the rifle upward, aiming at the ceiling. I fired two rounds into the apartment above me. The normally muffled *bang* sounded loud in the confines of the one-room apartment.

As I fired, out of the corner of one eye I saw a brief flash in the windows across the street. Acting out of a well-tuned sense of preservation, I dropped behind the dresser as two bullets tore into the wall behind where I had been standing. Huge rips appeared in the plaster.

I still had the rifle in my hands as I dropped to the floor, and as I had been trained at boot camp, I crawled on my belly until I was at the window behind the wall of sandbags. My heart raced and the skin of my arms and face were wet with perspiration, my hair glued to my forehead by sweat.

"Missed me again, pigs!" I called out. "You guys call yourselves snipers? What a fuckin' joke!"

I raised myself to my knees and set the rifle on the windowsill. I randomly selected one of the windows across the street, then fired two rounds into the dark-enshrouded room. I paused, keeping my breathing low, straining to detect any sounds indicating I'd hit something soft.

Gritting my teeth, I cursed under my breath.

Nothing.

A knock on the door made me freeze and my heart skipped a beat. Cops don't knock. I moved to stand to one side of the door, the gun held tightly to my chest.

I wasn't going down without a fight.

"Johnny, it's Wally," said a muffled voice that could be Wally Boxer.

And it might another trick. The enemy was devious.

It occurred to me that the cops were working with the VC.

They may have recruited a VC consultant to get to me.

I smiled to myself. Man, they were really desperate to stop me from speaking the truth.

"Okay, Wally. I'm here," I shouted, my harsh voice echoing off the walls.

"You need to come out," Wally said, or maybe the fake Wally.

My mind whirled with possible scenarios. "How do I know it's you?"

There was a pause for several seconds. "Listen, kid, I made a mistake tellin' you and Paddy to volunteer. I'm sorry. I wanta make it up to you. I have a special job for you."

The tension in my body eased and I sagged against the wall. I knew it had to be Wally Boxer. He knew about Paddy and me and his promise to us.

"How do we do this?" I asked.

"Put the gun down and come out with your hands on your head. The cops won't shoot. The captain and I are old friends. I made him promise."

Since most of the cops were on Wally's payroll, I believed him. I trusted him more than anyone in the world.

I leaned the rifle against the wall. Then I slipped the deadbolt aside to unlock the door. The hinges creaked as I swung it open, careful to keep the door between the hallway and me.

I sucked in a deep breath to steel myself for the lead that was going come at me, then locked my hands on my head and stepped through the open doorway.

I was preparing to die in the dimly lit hallway when a calloused, rough hand grabbed my right arm, yanked me forward off balance, then shoved me facedown on the floor. I landed hard on my belly, knocking the wind out of me. Spots danced before my eyes.

Through the haze of pain, I saw a pair of polished brown loafers approach me. I strained my head back and saw Wally standing over me in his brown, white and black checked pants and white short-sleeved dress shirt, his dead eyes studied me from his tanned round face. Worry lines furrowed his forehead.

"Hi, kid."

My hands were pulled roughly behind my back, making me wince. Next, cold steel surrounded my wrists, accompanied by the sound of handcuffs being locked. The steel cut into my wrists, adding to my discomfort.

"Wally," I croaked as a sense of relief washed over me. I wanted to laugh. "I'm gonna sing. I'm gonna tell the truth." Two sets hands grabbed my arms and raised me to my feet.

Wally shook his head as a small smile drifted over his lips. His eyes remained placid. "No, you're not, kid. You're gonna plead guilty to killin' those cops, then you're gonna be locked up for a long time."

I was shocked. "But I killed them others, too. The bastards need to be stopped before they murder all the kids."

Wally nodded and sighed. "Yeah, I know, kid. I understand. But we're gonna pin those murders on the Black Panthers. Those disloyal black scumbags need to be brought down."

A feeling of horror shot through me. They were using me and somehow they had gotten to my mentor, too. "But, Wally...why?"

Wally smirked. "Everyone's got an agenda, kid." The brief, unfeeling smile faded from his lips. "You'll keep quiet. And if you get outta the pen, I'll have a job waitin' for ya. Just like I promised."

"But what about the war...the senseless killing...the VC....What about Paddy?"

Wally's eyes flitted to mine. "Paddy's dead. You're alive. A shattered man to be sure but still among the living." He shrugged. "Life's unfair, what can I say?"

It occurred to me Wally had repaid me for his mistake by saving my life. I also knew if I didn't agree to his terms, I wouldn't make it to court.

I'd failed.

Tears began to steam down my cheeks.

I'd truly failed.

More guys would die and there was nothing that would prevent it happening.

Wally's last words to me before the pigs dragged me to the stairs were, "Don't worry, kid, you're still a loyal soldier. That's gotta count for somethin', right?"

About the Author

International selling author, Russ Crossley writes science fiction and fantasy, and mystery/suspense as well as their various subgenres.

His latest science fiction satire set in the far future, Revenge of the Lushites, is a sequel to Attack of the Lushites released in 2011. The latest title in the series was released in the fall of 2013. Both titles are available in e-book and trade paperback.

He has sold several short stories that have appeared in anthologies from various publishers including; WMG Publishing, Pocket Books, 53rd Street Publishing, and St. Martins Press.

He is a member of SF Canada and is past president of the Greater Vancouver Chapter of Romance Writers of America. He is also an alumni of the Oregon Coast Professional Fiction Writers Master Class taught by award winning author/editors, Kristine Katherine Rusch and Dean Wesley Smith.

Feel free to contact him on Facebook, Twitter, or his website http//:www.russcrossley.com. He loves to hear from readers.

Other titles from 53rd Street Publishing you may enjoy
http://www.53rdstreetpublising.com

Other books by the Author

Razor and Edge Mysteries
The Kidnapping of Billy Buttons
String of Pearls
Death by Clown
Beggin' For Murder
Ragged Ice
The Grand Central Mystery
A Strange Case of Undead Murder

Jazz Stiletto Mysteries
A Day Without Sunshine
Skullduggery
Instrument of justice (first published in Over My Dead Body online
mystery magazine)

The Amanda Dark paranormal mysteries
Hook Island
Grind Manor
Moonrise Diner
A Father's Daughter

The Trudy Wilson Mystery Novel Series
Bad Loyalty
Shear Murder
Buzzcut coming in 2015

Other Novels
Attack of the Lushites
Revenge of the Lushites

My Zombie Prince
Antique Virgin
The Fire In Their Hearts
with R.S. Meger (from Champagne Books)
Zomopolis
The Last Serial Killer

Short Stories
Countdown
Shoeless Moe
Round Up At The Burger Bar:
The Story of Trixie Pug, Parts 1, 2, 3, 4, 5, 6, 7, 8, 9
Five Minutes
Blossom Queen, Barbarian
The Secret
The Family Line
End of the Flies
Death by Magic
The Penguin Sleeps With The Fishes
Only The Worthy
Hero For A Day
End of Empire
Strange Bedfellows
Big Business
A Perfect Crime
The Wise Guy and The Pirates
In Search of the Perfect Cup
T.I.N. Men
The Legend of G and the Dragonettes
The Incredible Mr. Fix-It
Lock Stock and Barrel
Divided Loyalties
Cave of Wonders
A Family Empire
Until We Meet Again
Dragon Rising
Solitary Man

The Keel Mountain Conspiracy
Angel on My Shoulder
Heroes of Old
The Great Bicycle Race
Tikka's Big Day
"My Partner the Zombie" —
Hungry For Your Love Anthology
(St. Martin's Press)
Big Hairy Deal
One Red Shoe
A Bad Day in Lunden Texas
Bloody Betty, Queen of the Pirates
Mirror Image
Dangerous Waters
Cape Disappointment
Boomerang
The Watcher of Wayburn Street
The Apprentice
Drip!
A Beautiful Friendship and The Parrot of Doom
Robine's Diary
The Christmas Club
Loose Ends
Splatter Pattern
It Takes Two
Lexicon
Replacement Parts
Sidekicks
Lost Stories
Time and Space
Survivors
Neighborhood Watch
Unnatural Immortal
Rum Runner's Lounge
It's A Small Galaxy
A Shattered Man
Betrayed

Replacement Parts
Clubhouse Heroes
Sounds That Angels Make
Muggins Rules – originally published in Fiction River Volume 12,
Risk Takers

Anthologies
Tales of Urban Fantasy
Five Tales of Bizarre Detectives
Tales of Mystery and Suspense
Tales of Weird Fantasy
Spies, Detectives, & Heroes
Tales of Twisted Crime
Tales of The Unexpected
Tales From Space
10 by Russ Crossley
Round Up At The Burger Bar: The Story of Trixie Pug,
Parts 1- 5 The Beginning
Worlds of Science Fiction and Fantasy
More Tales of Mystery and Suspense
Ladies of the Jolly Roger
Justice Served
Love Stories
Ladies of the Jolly Roger with Rita Schulz
The Adventures of Razor and Edge:
Five Tales From The Quirky Detective Team
An Unexpected Journey
On Edge
Thrilling Adventures
Total War

Non-Fiction
The Writers Tools - The Synopsis

Another title from 53rd Street Publishing you may enjoy.

53rd Street Publishing invites you to Tales of the Fantastic, a five story collection of the finest fantasy from international selling author, Rita Schulz.

In the collection you will find stories of a tormented werewolf, sibling ghosts, fairies who need to help, and partying aliens.

So join us on a journey to wonder and amazement you won't want to miss.

www.ingramcontent.com/pod-product-compliance
Lightning Source LLC
Chambersburg PA
CBHW020545130626
46552CB00007B/2765